# MRS. HENSWORTHY'S BOOKCASE

*A Tale of Science Fiction, Served with*
*Tea and Biscuits*

*By*

# Norman J Barta

BALINOR BOOKS
2024

## Manufactured in the United States of America

ISBN Number: 979-8-9891371-5-2 (Hardback)
ISBN Number: 979-8-9891371-6-9 (Paperback)
Also available as an eBook

Library of Congress Control Number: 2024903993

Balinor Books, a division of Balinor International, llc, is a boutique publishing house domiciled in the United States.

*Enjoy these other fine works from Balinor Books, now available at Amazon.com!*

## The Continuing Adventures of Sir Roderick Melrose
*A titillating erotic romance and humorous travel adventure in the Victorian vernacular*

## The Conversational Poet
*Love, wit and wisdom celebrated in the joy of verse*

## A Little Jaunt through Scandinavia, or
*Norman and Lisa's Nordic Adventure in The Year of Our Volvo 2001*

## About the author:

I always find it curious that these "About the Author" paragraphs are prepared in the third person; I believe everyone knows that this completely flattering and immodest description is inevitably prepared by the author himself, herself, itself, or whatever particular –self the author prefers.

That said, I try to aspire to justifying the title of "Renaissance Personage." Vocationally, I'm an entrepreneur trying to bring about exciting device-driven changes in the realm of medical care. Avocationally, I'm an author, poet, architect, artist, cabinet-maker, musician.

Feel free to peruse *www.njbarta.com* for a peek at some of the pursuits that float my proverbial boat (although I might mention that boating is not necessarily one of those pursuits).

And please enjoy the journey!

# MRS. HENSWORTHY'S BOOKCASE

# 1

Mrs. Eleanora Hensworthy was enjoying a cup of tea in her sitting room. She particularly relished these respites on those cool afternoons when a comforting fire occupied the fireplace, with the chairs and sofa placed before it so as to ensure a good dose of warmth from the hearth.

As she looked around the room, she enjoyed the view of the birds through the large window on the wall opposite her comfy chair. She also enjoyed contemplating the large bookcase one could access by walking behind the sofa. It was actually a walk-through bookcase, providing access to her kitchen in the next room. It was formed by two bookcases, joined by a bridge of shelving above the doorway. Of course, she could always enter the kitchen by a second doorway from the entry hall, but she felt it was rather magical walking through that bookcase. The bookcase had been designed and constructed by her dearly departed husband Malthorp; at least, that's how Mrs. Hensworthy always referred to him. It garnered for her a great deal of sympathy. He hadn't actually died, of course; he had just decided to depart one day for points unknown. She often wondered where he had wandered off to, but quickly shrugged off such thoughts and returned to her tasks or her tea.

As she sat sipping periodically from her cup and enjoying her surroundings, she heard an odd sound, a sound with which she was unfamiliar. It was a whooshing sort of sound, rather like an overanxious vacuum cleaner, if a vacuum cleaner could in fact be overanxious. It grew to be annoyingly loud, and she was considering complaining once again to the neighbors, if indeed the sound was originating from their locale on this occasion. They were often making various loud noises about which Mrs. Hensworthy chose to complain, but the noise was definitely more localized this time.

It was then that she noticed something extremely odd. There was a little dot in the middle of the bookcase doorway. It sort of just hung there in the air, like a tennis ball suspended on a string, although there was neither a tennis ball nor any string evident. Slowly, it grew larger, and Mrs. Hensworthy could now discern a view of some sort of objects going to and fro; or perhaps it was more like looking through a tiny tennis-ball-like window, although now it was more like the size of a basketball.  It continued to grow, and one would have thought that Mrs. Hensworthy would have displayed some sign of shock or amazement at this turn of events, but she continued to serenely enjoy her tea as she observed the proceedings.  She hadn't seen this sort of thing before, but she was loath to mention anything unusual to any of her nosy neighbors.  They already thought that her proverbial bulb was on the flicker after she mentioned to them that the local sheep herd had recently warned her most emphatically about some coming weather.  She didn't need them dwelling any further on the subject of her intellectual capacities.

The enigma finally stopped growing; it was about the size of the bookcase opening now, a decently sized doorway that sort of whorled fuzzily about at the edges, and Mrs.

Hensworthy could clearly see that people, or perhaps something other than people, were moving past the opening, as if hurriedly going about their shopping. She was continuing to enjoy her tea, with that delightfully toasty fire keeping her toes warm, when there was the most extraordinary occurrence.

# 2

Brobding Measelfort was an exceptionally diligent employee of the MITE Corporation. Whenever a breach was reported in one of the company's many transdimensional transport tubes, Brobding Measelfort would conscientiously rush to the scene with the tools and materials needed to solve the problem. These breaches seemed to occur more and more often these days, filling Brobding Measelfort's days as he ran from place to place effecting repairs.

MITE, officially known about the neighborhood as the Mdoaaertjofagsdbzzfgsiodfnlmklidrtr Interstellar Transit Express Corporation, managed the transdimensional transport system that allowed for plentiful commerce among the many planets in the local galaxy. Of course, everyone referred to the company as MITE, as the actual name was rather a pain to pronounce, even for the most literate and well-spoken species. As for humans, who were as yet unaware of transdimensional transport facilities, should they have tried to pronounce the company's name properly, their tongues would thereafter require major surgical repair (except, perhaps, those of Welsh ancestry, who are quite skilled in pronouncing terms of this sort), and even then, they would have ongoing difficulty pronouncing the letter d.  It was somewhat odd that the company should be named MITE, as coincidentally, the species who serviced the MITE passages appeared rather like large, well, mites.  Actually, from a human perspective, one supposes that "enormous 16-legged bedbug" would be a more apt description of these beings, but, as humans were not yet part of the transdimensional equation, the term "mite" serves our purposes as an apt descriptor.

Brobding Measelfort was one such being.  As I'm sure many of you recognized immediately, he was from the planet known as Measel, as were many of his fellow transport tube repair workers.  Just as a matter of proseful housekeeping, we shall use the human pronouns "he" or "she" when the need arises to refer to various beings, because each planet has a variety of such pronouns, and this would become quite confusing as we refer to one species or another. Brobding Measelfort was actually a "zhayabenoing," but, as this has no meaning to humans, we'll stick with "he."

It was a relatively easy task to identify those beings who called the planet Measel their home. Firstly, there were of course the 16 appendages and rather bedbug-like appearance. To the untrained eye, all Measeloots (which is how one refers to those from Measel) might look alike, but of course, Measeloots easily distinguished one from another among themselves, particularly as they had excellent vision in the far ultraviolet end of the color spectrum, and displayed a variety of interesting colors in that range upon their appendages.

A second manner in which to distinguish a Measeloot was that each of them had the term "measel" somewhere in their names. Brobding Measelfort is an excellent example, as are his rather overbearing aunt on his mother's side, Measelanna Hooscod, and his favorite first cousin, Willodig Propmeasel.

Measeloots are considered among the most congenial species in the immediate galactic neighborhood; a slang term has even been coined accordingly in referring to those of a friendly and helpful nature, as in, "He's quite a measel sort, isn't he?" Or, "I've always found her to be reasonably measel."

The MITE Corporation was headquartered on Lechien 7, purportedly so named because its inhabitants sounded, to the unpracticed ear, rather like yapping dogs when they spoke. The planet had also been nicknamed the Annoying Yorkie Planet, for the same reason. Luckily, the use of a GadgiYack, worn decoratively in any convenient nostril, automatically translated language heard among the various species, among which the benefits included a greatly improved degree of sociability at interspecies cocktail parties. It was important, however, that both individuals in a discussion take advantage of a GadgiYack, as absence thereof would make for a rather one-sided conversation.

Today was an important day at the MITE Corporation, keeping in mind that, from a human perspective, a "day" on Lechien 7 was 57.61 earth hours long, which made for some exceptional all-night soirees. The MITE board was meeting to discuss the transdimensional concrete situation.

As you may be aware, the price of transdimensional concrete had gone up quite dramatically in recent times, what with the consolidation of both the transdimensional concrete manufacturers and quarkonite mining companies. In case you forgot, let me remind you that quarkonite is a key ingredient in transdimensional concrete. There were at one time 877 transdimensional concrete companies and 512 quarkonite mining enterprises in the local galaxy, not including the small black market operations. Now, with the usual gobbling up of competitors over time, only six concrete companies and three mining operations dominate the field, and there were rumors of price collusion among the remaining suppliers.

In addition, the costs associated with mining quarkonite are quite out of hand. As you know, the mining operations have been experiencing a particularly annoying occurrence of small singularities, causing the occasional shoe and a variety of socks (and, it seems, always the one sock of a pair) to disappear into these voids. While the shoe manufacturers publically commiserate with the mine operators with respect to these losses, everyone who's anyone is quite certain that the shoemakers are quietly celebrating in the background, as shoe sales have increased markedly. We'll be joining the MITE board meeting at an important juncture.

Mayrile Flernk, a Chienolian and one of the more senior and vocal board members, spoke (or barked, as the case may be) right up. As a point of interest, it was often irritating to listen to Mayrile's shrill manner of expression, but his acquaintances tolerated it because he was often known to pick up the check at dinner. "Well, my fellow boardians, what are we to do about this concrete situation? The prices are becoming outrageous. That, combined with all the breach occurrences we've been seeing of late, is going to start affecting our bottom line, and we can't keep raising tolls on the transdimensional tubes. The smaller traders are already barking that the tolls are seriously cutting into their margins. If everyone starts raising prices because of toll increases, we'll never hear the end of it, and the planetary governments will get involved, especially since elections are coming up on at least twelve planets in the trading league. The incumbents are going to explode if they face inflationary pressures in an election cycle! Thoughts?"

Meelus Permeaselputt, another respected board member (and I bet you know what planet he comes from!), had a thought. "Perhaps we might consider vertically integrating? If we controlled the concrete and mining operations, we wouldn't be as worried about these costs."

A murmur arose around the room, and Mayrile Flernk addressed the possibilities. "Well, Meelus, in theory, that would put us in the dunkbot's seat, but let's consider the cases. Transdimensional concrete manufacturing is a dirty business, and you know the flack the current manufacturers have been getting lately about polluting their star systems. On top of that, there are some huge infrastructure costs to break into that business." More murmuring ensued.

"As for quarkonite mining, need I remind everyone of the Halcyon Mine Incident?" Mayrile looked around, saw a few nods, and heard a few clicks. "All right, I'll remind you, then. Halycon was developing a rich vein of charmed quarks when, before you could say 'down and strange,' BOOM! Two mining planets and my favorite vacation asteroid, gone. No, my friends, while it might offer some price security, I don't think verticality is the answer. Porlot, any contributions?"

Porlot Wheezleween was the Executive Golgot of the MITE Corporation; responsibility for the company's bottom line ultimately came back to her. Porlot was from the Kor group of planets, circling a binary star system. Upon casual perusal, Porlot looked like a fairly substantial version of those annoying little balls that fall off the sweet gum trees every autumn. Korpits (which is how one refers collectively to the inhabitants of Kor) are more or less spherical, and short appendages protruded rather symmetrically about the sphere. There seemed to be eyes, and what one might interpret as ears, everywhere, in addition to no less than four orifices, each of which might qualify as a mouth.

She had worked her way up through the ranks from toll taker, satisfying most of the company's job descriptions along the way, and had been listening carefully to the conversation. "I want to know why we're having so many breaches in the first place! I'm going to assemble a task force and try to find out what's going on. In the meantime, I'd like to suggest we negotiate some longer term supply contracts with the transdimensional concrete companies; I can't see the prices coming down any time soon." There was a general rumble of approval within the assembled group.

Mayrile Flernk jumped in, figuratively speaking. "It's decided, then. Porlot will pursue studies on the one hand as to the cause of these confounded breaches, and on the other hand, will start contacting the concrete suppliers to try and control our costs. In the meantime, I suggest we keep our tolls as they are, to avoid any unnecessary interest on the part of meddling government officials." The group nodded, clicked and whistled in agreement, and the meeting adjourned.

# 3

Pyrheos Fourthinline was hired to do a job. He was from the planet known as Wokwok Secondinline, which had some rather unusual approaches when it came to assigning the family name.

Pyrheos was an investigator for the MITE Corporation, and was recently tasked with getting to the root of all these transdimensional tube breaches that had been occurring throughout the system. One section was being particularly troublesome, involving tubes adjacent to a star system in one of the outer arms. While the breaches had involved only the inner wall of the tube so far, these had occurred in the vicinity of Barnork 3 (or what the humans refer to as Earth), and the trading league had no interest in having humans enter the fray at the present time, as they found humans to be far too primitive, erratic and violent to be participating in interstellar trade.

Perhaps they'd be allowed to join if they ever showed some signs of maturing.

The breaches were becoming more frequent, with larger and larger openings evident. The scientific community had recently expressed its concerns that an "interdimensional merge" might occur as a result of these events, with unknown consequences, as this had never happened before, at least unintentionally.

After investigating for some time, Pyrheos was ready to provide a preliminary report. He contacted the home office, and was connected to one of Porlot Wheezleween's primary sound receptors.

Pyrheos was impressed; most employees would be connected to a tertiary sound receptor, or perhaps a secondary sound receptor at best. Their comments would only be elevated to the Primary Brain Section if a priority had been established with respect to the subject matter.

Pyrheos heard one of Porlot's vocal orifices clear its proverbial throat. "So tell me, Fourthinline, what have you found so far."

Pyrheos answered somewhat nervously, as he had never before spoken directly with an Executive Golgot.

"Well, Executive Wheezleween, my preliminary findings would tend to indicate that these breaches are not of a natural origin; that is, it's my opinion that these breaches are being systematically introduced to the system. I've also been reviewing the breach records, and I think I can say most definitively that the breaches are becoming larger and more frequent with the passage of local time, taking into account the various interdimensional time variations."

Porlot was quick with her response. "What evidence leads you to the conclusion that these breaches are intentional?"

Pyrheos had anticipated this one. "There is a certain consistency in the shape and depth of the breaches. You'll note from the data that there has not yet been a catastrophic interdimensional penetration; only a weakening of the wall. And the weakening is in a fairly consistent, almost circular shape each time."

Porlot digested this information. "All right, Fourthinline, good work so far. How would you suggest we proceed?"

"I would like to suggest, if possible of course, Executive Wheezleween, that we place some observational orbitons in the tubes, to see if we can't capture the miscreants on hologram."

Porlot cringed. "It's probably a good idea, but we've tried placing some orbitons in the past, and every time we do that, we hear from the patrons who are, shall we say, more sensitive to being observed, and they proceed to contact their local governments. The next thing you know, I'm being harassed by various planetary representatives, being accused of Big Bortle-ism, and they're throwing references my way to that dystopian book *4891*. I really don't need the hassle!"

There was silence between them as they considered the alternatives; Porlot had a thought. "I'll tell you what; I was just shown the new Model ON-76776 orbiton, which seems to be much flatter and less conspicuous than the old 64633 model. See if you can get your hands on some of the new ones, and place a handful where you think they might be useful. Also, set them to go fully flat during the busy transit hours, to reduce the likelihood of complaints; I have a feeling that, if these breaches are on purpose, they're being introduced when the tubes are mostly unoccupied."

Both parties were satisfied with this next step, and Pyrheos went about his business.

# 4

"I've reviewed the orbiton information, and have something to report." Pyrheos was excited.

Porlot was once again listening with one of her primary sound receptors, while she pursued four other important tasks. "What do you have for me, Fourthinline?"

Pyrheos brought up a holographic image for them to review. "We captured this image of someone introducing a breach."

Porlot swiveled several eyes in the direction of the hologram. "What is that they're holding? Is that a portable collider?!"

"Yes, I believe it is. I think they're using it to produce a micro-singularity and suck up some transdimensional material from the wall of the tube. They're probably capturing the singularity in a magnetic field after that for later disposal somewhere else."

"Any luck identifying the perpetrator?" Porlot was getting excited.

Pyrheos looked a little sad. "No, I'm afraid whoever it is seems to have some sort of covering. It may also be protective gear. If you look closely, that appears to be one of those cheap particle colliders you can pick up at any sleazy corner fusion shop, and I don't need to tell you, a leaking particle collider can be real trouble. I can get a better magnetic field from my pet dordle than you get from one of those gadgets!" Pyrheos made a sound that one might interpret as a chuckle. "Sorry, off the subject. Notice the four feet; it's a little hard to make out, but I would say it looks to me like 14 toes in front, 8 in back on each foot."

Porlot looked pensive; she spoke slowly. "Huh. A Narl. Now what would a Narl have against the MITE Corporation?"

Pyrheos thought for a moment. "Well, remember when the Transdimensional Transit Tube was first opened to the Narls? There was a group on the planet that made a particularly effective fungal foot powder. I remember hearing a lot of complaints because they had a monopoly on it, and the prices were getting out of hand. And Narls seem to have a lot of trouble with foot fungus."

Porlot nodded. "I'm not surprised, what with a humid atmosphere, swampy conditions, and 88 toes to worry about."

Pyrheos nodded, and continued, "Shortly after the Narls gained access to interstellar trade, Burgeonos 6 offered them a similar product at a much better price. With 100 appendages and six toes on each appendage, the Bergeons were experts on the subject of foot fungus. In any case, the monopoly kind of fell apart at that point, so it might be that the Narls are trying to protect their home planet monopoly."

Porlot looked incredulous. "Foot fungus powder?! These breaches are about foot fungus powder?! Oh, bortle, now I've heard everything! All right, I'm going to see if I can get the Narls in for a discussion, and hopefully we can reach some kind of agreement. Yikes! In the meantime, Fourthinline, good work, and keep an eye on the orbiton output to see if we can get some more definitive data. If this was just about the Narls, I don't think we'd be seeing breaches the way we are, all throughout the system."

The following week (at least in terms of Lechien 7), before Porlot Wheezleween could arrange a meeting with the Narls, a message arrived at MITE headquarters. It was immediately brought to Porlot's attention. And not just Porlot's attention, but to the attention of her Primary Brain Section. This was important.

She perused the contents, and immediately reached out to Pyrheos Fourthinline. "I was just presented with a threatening message. You'd better see this, Fourthinline; it explains a lot."

Pyrheos made his way to Porlot's locale, and similarly surveyed the note:

*We the Planetarials will continue in our efforts to discourage use of the transdimensional tubes for commerce, as we feel that our own planetary suppliers should be given precedence over "foreign" supply sources. You can expect the breaches to continue and worsen until you close the tubes.*

Porlot watched Pyrheos as he absorbed the implications. "Well, Fourthinline, what do you think?"

Pyrheos considered what he had just seen. "I think this is about quite a bit more than foot fungus powder. Have you heard of these Planetarials? And do we have any source on this message, or any idea who else might be involved?"

"I think that's your department, Fourthinline. See what you can find out, and we'll try to negotiate with the key players and reach some kind of agreement. There are a whole lot of tube patrons who will be really, really angry if we need to close the transit corridors.

In the meantime, we'll need to increase security in the tubes, and try to stop these blasted breaches! And I'm going to get in touch with an academic friend of mine who can shed some light on the implications if these breaches get any worse."

# 5

As Professor of Multidimensional Physics at Lechien 7's Center for Education in the Galactic Sciences, Lorkin Lort knew his way around the dimensional block. He was one of the key figures in mapping the interdimensional folds that formed the very foundation of the transdimensional transport network. This of course brought to life the MITE Corporation, and allowed commerce to move from one planet to another with essentially the same ease as travelers had earlier enjoyed in moving from town to town on their own planets.

Lorkin had some history with Porlot Wheezleween. In their long-ago youths, they had met at the Advanced Educational Center on Rangus, a planet renowned as a citadel of learning. Lorkin and Porlot had enjoyed certain other pleasures together as well, thanks in part to the aphrodisiac nature of the atmosphere on Rangus (which made studying quite the challenge), but ultimately decided to go their separate ways. While Porlot continued to enjoy the occasional tryst here and there, Lorkin had settled on one mate, and produced 6 little Lorts.

Their friendship continued to the present day. So when Lorkin was contacted by Porlot, it was nothing out of the ordinary.

"Greetings, Porlot, I trust you're maintaining the machinery of commerce in sound working order?"

Porlot wore a concerned expression. "Hi, Lorkin. To respond to your question, yes and no."

It was Lorkin's turned to look concerned. "You haven't thrown a toodlewrench into the works of my transdimensional network, have you?" He attempted a weak smile.

Porlot dived right in. "No, Lorkin, nothing like that. We have some nasty sorts who we believe are using colliders to create micro-singularities, which then deteriorate the walls of our transdimensional tubes. They call themselves the Planetarials.  So I have a few questions."

Now Lorkin's concerns were genuine.  "I don't need to tell you, Porlot, wall failures are no laughing matter.  As I haven't seen any reports of catastrophe lately, I can only assume you haven't had any true rifts in the tubes."

"Not so far; but the way things are going, it's only a matter of time if we can't bring these attacks under control."  Porlot continued, "We've had wall intrusions throughout the network, with a cluster of issues in the vicinity of the Barnork system."

Lorkin began to tick off the important talking points on the subject.  "Well you know the drill as well as I do, Porlot.  The tubes are tricky to generalize; some longer than others, and they transit various environments.  Multidimensional or not, if we were to get a breakthrough rift in a wall exposed to void, we're going to get atmospheric evacuation.  Not pretty.  We had enough problems contending with atmospheric inflows and outflows as we opened each portal at the planetary level; luckily, end point locks can keep that under control when needed.  But with a rift, the locks won't help. As for the Barnork system, you have another problem there. We have the Grange planetary system in 3-space 784 that overlaps the Barnork system in... I believe it's been identified as 3-space 1022. It doesn't happen often, but there you have it. If I remember correctly, based on the interdimensional folds in that region, I believe the Grange system accesses at least two transdimensional tubes for trade. What with the planetary systems overlapping, a breach in that region could expose the tube network to inhabitants on the Barnork planets. I don't believe they're part of the network as yet, are they?"

Porlot looked weary. "No, and we want to keep it that way; from the reports I've seen from a scientific expedition to that area, the inhabitants are still quite primitive and hostile. It's taken us a long time to get rid of the jerks in the various dimensions we deal with now, and we're still not done with that, though at this point everyone's pretty much managed to mature past their violent tendencies. The Barnork dwellers aren't there yet. Any recommendations?"

Lorkin thought briefly. "Porlot, all I can suggest is the obvious; get a resolution to any conflict involving breaches, and get it in place as fast as possible. In the meantime, do your best to keep your tubes in good repair. You might also consider closing the particular tubes where a breach would pose the greatest issue, but I know your patrons and shareholders won't be too keen on that. By the way, if you still have that report on the Barnork system, may I impose on you to send it over? I'd like to review it."

"Not a problem, Lorkin. The report is on the way. I was hoping you'd have better news for me, though."

Lorkin smiled. "I warned you that MITE would give you a pain when you took the job. Sorry I can't be more helpful, but there it is. I wish you the best, Porlot."

Shortly thereafter, Lorkin received the report, "*Clandestine Sociological and Psychological studies of the Barnork System Inhabitants.*" Suddenly, he looked concerned once again. He joined his colleague, Professor Beelox Dromdon, for a discussion on the contents.

"I'm trusting my friend Porlot Wheezleween to ensure we don't have any dimensional breaches into this Barnork system. I don't think we really want to deal with those folks, I believe they use the term 'humans,' from Barnork 3, known colloquially as Earth. They actually believe," and he started to laugh, "in something they call," he hesitated, laughing too vigorously at the moment to continue, "I can hardly say it....the Big Bang Theory!" The two of them were laughing now. "And, wait for it...," he continued, "dark matter!" They were now rolling around the room with laughter.

Beelox managed to speak up between bouts of hysteria. "Stop, stop, you're killing me! I'm going to plork right here if you keep it up!"

The laughter gradually died down. "Oh, my, it's good to have a laugh like that once in a while," Beelox continued. "How can they not see the Interdimensional Model? It's so much more elegant than, what do they call it, the Big Bang Theory? I saw that the fellow who assembled the report referred to it as 'Theological Astrophysics.'"

Lorkin had calmed down also. "I have a theory on that. I think that, because their perception is rather primitive, and limited to a particular 3-space, they can't seem to grasp the true implications of N-space and the interdimensional transition of matter. Or, for that matter, no pun intended, that the matter they see in their 3-space may in fact be a 3-dimensional projection or shadow of matter originating in N-space."

"For example, they seem to think everything they see just magically started from a point, and, BOOM, was suddenly everywhere, hence, Big Bang. They don't understand how matter might transition from N-space to 3-space in what they perceive as a 3-dimensional globular fashion through an infinitesimal dimensional rift. Or even the simple concept of the 3-dimensional projection of N-space matter into their 3-space, thereby acting as the gravitational driver that explains what they see as 'expansion.' The report said that some of their ilk were sort of on the right track. Hopefully one day they'll figure it out. I would say it's time for a drink."

# 6

Brobding Measelfort was not a fan of the outer rim locales. It was tiring getting there, as you had to access several transdimensional tubes in the right sequence to reach your desired destination. Brobding found the journey rather tedious.

And it seemed he was spending more and more time in this vicinity, what with all the breaches to be found here. The big bosses at MITE still hadn't reached any useful resolution with the Planetarials and their isolationist demands, and the Planetarials had become, if possible, even more militant, opening larger and larger breaches more and more often. Some of the planetary governments were considering instituting tariffs to protect their home industries and hopefully satisfy the Planetarials, but the free trade sorts were pushing back, and the parties were at somewhat of a stalemate.

Brobding had a bad feeling about these breaches; he thought that it was only a matter of time before something really serious happened.

Brobding made his way along one of the transdimensional tubes used to access the Grange planetary system in 3-space 784. Grange 5 and 6 had some of the best restaurants in this part of the galaxy, and Brobding thought that perhaps he'd take advantage of that and grab a bite as soon as he finished his next repair.

He reached the reported breach locale; it was a particularly nasty more-or-less circular failure in the tube wall. As with the other breaches to which he'd been attending of late, this one affected the inner wall, but did not constitute an interdimensional rift. Brobding hadn't experienced one of those as yet, and thought it would be just fine with him if he never saw a true rift during his tenure as a repair technician. He took out his tools, and began to prepare a batch of transdimensional concrete. As I'm sure you're aware, it has to have just the right quarkonite content to ensure a proper interdimensional seal; otherwise, the particle charges would be all wrong, and the concrete would lose all cohesion in pretty short order. There was no cause for concern here, however; by now, Brobding Measelfort was an expert when it came to the recipe for transdimensional concrete.

He completed his preparations, and was ready to apply the mixture.    Of a sudden, as he began to trowel on the transdimensional concrete in an effort to patch the breach, Brobding Measelfort accidentally broke through the wall of the transdimensional transport tube, and was left standing (or in a position one might interpret as standing, given his 16 appendages) in what turned out to be Mrs. Hensworthy's living room.

This was certainly a new experience for him; the wall of a tube had never fully given way before, and Brobding Measelfort had no idea where he was.  He surveyed the scene, and espied Mrs. Hensworthy and her niece Gwendolyn standing before him, their mouths agape and a look of absolute terror on their faces.

As a little background, Mrs. Hensworthy had asked her niece Gwendolyn to visit, so that someone other than Mrs. Hensworthy would actually witness the events unfolding in her living room. Mrs. Hensworthy grew weary of the accusations and innuendoes of her acquaintances with respect to her "playing with a full deck," and was sure Gwendolyn's own observations would put such nonsense to rest.

Gwendolyn was a young woman of 22, though she still thought of herself in many ways as a teen. She worked as a waitress at The Bountiful Bazonga, a dining establishment in the big city that took pride in the physical attributes of its wait staff. There was a certain consistent clientele that similarly appreciated those attributes.

Like an artist pleased to display her favorite works, Gwendolyn had a tendency to wear short skirts and rather form fitting tops that left little to the imagination.

They had been standing in her living room, observing the odd formation in the doorway of Mrs. Hensworthy's impressive walk-through bookcase, when Brobding Measelfort made his unfortunate appearance.

Thanks to Brobding Measelfort's GadgiYack translator device, he could understand Mrs. Hensworthy and Gwendolyn perfectly, and the ladies were offering plenty of agitated commentary upon experiencing Brobding's presence in their home. Unfortunately, as they had yet to acquire GadgiYacks of their own, Brobding Measelfort was so far completely unintelligible to the ladies. As he was a most congenial sort, and certainly desirous of communicating with them in the most friendly manner to determine where he was and how this terrible rift had happened, he attempted to remedy the situation.

Reaching back through the rift, Brobding took a spare GadgiYack from his tool box. He then tried to find a convenient nostril in either lady, in which to place the device. As he was quite unacquainted with human anatomy, he took hold of Gwendolyn and placed the device in what he thought was the most likely location for a nostril. It was not a nostril.

Gwendolyn squealed rather like a startled member of the porcine clan, and leapt back from Brobding's grasp. "I've heard about you aliens and your perverted probing! Keep away from me!" she exclaimed as she ran around the sofa. Brobding was not to be discouraged, however. He held up several appendages in what he perceived to be a sign of peace, and moved with conviction toward Mrs. Hensworthy.

Before the woman could get out of his way, Brobding Measelfort actually managed to place a GadgiYack in what turned out to be a nostril, and asked her to please, please calm herself.

Mrs. Hensworthy acquired a look of shock and delight on her face as the words registered in her brain. "My goodness, I understood what this giant bug just said!" Brobding Measelfort tried not to take the 'giant bug' reference personally. Gwendolyn looked on, still in shock, with a look of bewilderment.

Mrs. Hensworthy turned to her niece. "Gwendolyn, dear, you really must let this, mmmm, creature place one of these doodads in your nose; it's quite amazing!" As she spoke, Brobding Measelfort, having now definitively determined the location of the human nostril, quickly slipped a GadgiYack into place on

Gwendolyn, and proceeded to assure her that he was merely here to repair a leak, and meant no harm.

Despite the fact that she now understood Brobding perfectly, Gwendolyn hadn't quite recovered from her earlier experience with the GadgiYack. She tore the newly placed device from her nose, ran for the door, threw it open, and went screaming down the local lane.

Mrs. Hensworthy watched briefly as Gwendolyn disappeared from view. As she closed the door, she turned back to Brobding Measelfort; given his anatomy, she couldn't quite interpret his expression, but "surprise and confusion" were certainly somewhere in the mix.

Brobding was the first to speak. "Sorry to be a bother, but this is rather a first for me. Allow me to introduce myself; I'm Brobding Measelfort; can you perhaps tell me where I am?"

Mrs. Hensworthy resumed her chair near the fire. "Well, Mister….oh, I do beg your pardon, I'm presuming you're a mister, for lack of a better term, but in any case, it's lovely to meet you, Mr. Measelfort; I'm Mrs. Hensworthy. As for our locale, dear, you're in the village of Hampsthwaite. I realize it's a fairly small village; you may be better acquainted with Harrogate, a few miles down the lane."

Brobding didn't find this particularly helpful. "It is lovely to meet you, Mrs. Hensworthy, and I apologize for the intrusion. Perhaps I didn't phrase my earlier question particularly well. It would be helpful if you could tell me the planet upon which we're currently residing, or at least the particular star system."

Considering the question, Mrs. Hensworthy appeared surprisingly unperturbed. "Why, you're on Earth, dear. I'm not sure how to describe the... what was it you said? The star system? But if I remember my school science...my goodness, that was some time ago now....I believe it's commonly referred to as the Solar System. And say no more about intrusions! I welcome a bit of exotic company!"

Brobding wasn't getting anywhere; he had never heard of this Earth, and it certainly wasn't one of the planets serviced by the MITE Corporation. "Thank you for the information you've provided, Mrs. Hensworthy. If you would excuse me for just a moment, perhaps I can call my headquarters and get some clarification."

Brobding once again reached through the rift, and retrieved a small device that he placed in one of his four ears. With the series of signal amplifiers installed in the transdimensional tubes, interplanetary communication had taken off in a big way. Brobding connected to the home office on Lechien 7.

"This is Brobding Measelfort; I'm in the process of repairing a breach in tube 393483750433 of the Grange System. I've experienced something a little unusual; the breach has fully penetrated the tube, and become an interdimensional rift, and I sort of fell through. I'm speaking with one of the locals, a Mrs. Hensworthy, and she tells me I'm on the planet Earth, in what she refers to as the Solar System. I don't believe that's one of the planets we service; can someone there clarify exactly where I am at the moment? Also, unless you say otherwise, I presume I repair this breach the same way as any other breach."

Porlot Wheezleween's tertiary sound receptor rather absentmindedly monitored all the incoming technical traffic at the MITE Corporation, listening for anything that might be worthy of her attention. The word "rift" qualified as worthy. The data was immediately transferred to her Primary Brain Section. She interrupted the conversation.

"This is Porlot Wheezleween; did you just say 'rift'?"

Brobding Measelfort began to lightly vibrate; he had never spoke to the Executive Golgot before. He was a little nervous. "Ummm, yes, I sort of fell through a hole in the tube wall."

It was Porlot's turn to vibrate. "Stay right there, Measelfort; I'm sending a few interested parties to join you. Don't do anything until they get there. Understood?"

Brobding nodded. "Understood. Can you tell me where I am, though?"

Porlot was already contacting Lorkin Lort at the Center for Education in the Galactic Sciences. "The parties I'm sending will clarify everything for you. Just stay calm, and try to keep the situation under control."

Brobding wasn't sure what Porlot meant by 'under control;' Mrs. Hensworthy seemed like quite a friendly being. But he reassured Porlot in any case: "Will do."

# 7

Porlot was seriously agitated. This was big. Really, really big.

She connected with Lorkin Lort, and described the current situation.

He was silent for a moment. He spotted his colleague Beelox Dromdon in the distance and waved him over as he reacted to the news. "Porlot! Let's stay calm here! Nothing to get too frantic about!! Has there been any atmospheric venting? Is there a noticeable differential in matter volume at the point of rift that might cause significant movement through the rift? Tell me what's happening, Porlot!!"

It was clearly Lorkin who was excited.

"Calm yourself, Lorkin! And for Zeelot's sake, stop yelling! Everything's under control....so far." Porlot was somewhat annoyed that Lorkin was getting so emotional about a rift. "I'm sending you the coordinates of the tube breach; I thought you'd like to get to the scene as quickly as possible and evaluate the situation for yourself."

"Good, good! I'll assemble a small team and get right out there! Good thinking, Porlot!" Lorkin was doing the emotional thing again, and Porlot wasn't having it.

"Listen, Lorkin, you need to get it together. We already have an inhabitant from Barnork 3, something called a Missus Hensworthy, interacting with our Measel on the scene, Brobding Measelfort. Hopefully, Measelfort has offered the creature a GadgiYack so we can at least communicate with it. I don't know about this particular being's temperament, but you saw the report on the Barnork system; generally not the most welcoming sort. While you're in transit, I'll have Research see if we have any data on this Missus Hensworthy species."

"When you get there, I know you; your four brains are going to be completely captivated by the existence of a rift. But try to be as diplomatic as you can, Lorkin! We don't need an interdimensional incident here. If these creatures from Barnork get into the system, I'll never hear the end of it from planetary regulators all over the network!"

Lorkin was only half listening as he collected some instruments he wanted to bring along. As for Porlot's last sentence, Lorkin only heard the word 'end.' "Good, good, let's end the conversation here; I'll contact you when I'm at the location with my colleagues!" And with that he was gone.

Porlot felt tired after that call, and proceeded to contemplate the situation. "I hope he was listening to me. Sometimes Lorkin's brains are just all over the place! Measelfort didn't seem particularly agitated when we communicated earlier, so I think it's safe to assume we don't have any serious osmotic matter- or atmospheric-transfers going on. Now let's see what Research has to say about this Missus Hensworthy species."

An amazingly short while later, back at the rift, Lorkin Lort arrived with an entourage of three scientific types, including his colleague Beelox Dromdon. He hadn't lost any of his excitement. He and his associates stood in the transdimensional tube, and looked with overwhelming curiosity through the hole in the wall in front of them.  Brobding Measelfort caught a glimpse of them in his right-most eye, and turned to greet them.

"You must be the party mentioned to me by Executive Wheezleween; I'm...."

Lorkin was too impatient to wait for Brobding's introduction.  "Yes, yes, you're obviously Brobding Measelfort; Porlot said I should expect to find you here.  This is very exciting for us, Brobding!  Tell us, how exactly did this rift occur?"

Brobding was once again interrupted, this time by Mrs. Hensworthy.  "I must say, Mr. Measelfort, your friends seem to be in quite the hurry.  Perhaps introductions are in order?"

Brobding turned from one party to the other; he was in a bit of a quandary, as Lorkin was clearly anxious to determine the circumstances surrounding the formation of the rift, and was representing the interests of Executive Wheezleween.  On the other appendage, he didn't want to be impolite to Mrs. Hensworthy, who was more or less the hostess in this instance. He suggested to Lorkin that perhaps, given there didn't appear to be any particular emergency apparent as regarded the rift, it might be more diplomatic to accede to Mrs. Hensworthy's wishes, and introduce themselves.

"Of course, of course, Brobding. I'm pleased to see the being has a GadgiYack, so I'll proceed. I'm Lorkin Lort, Professor of Multidimensional Physics at The Center for Education in the Galactic Sciences on Lechien 7, and these are my esteemed colleagues, Beelox Dromdon, Waller Extork Whichkel, and Waller's able assistant, Nalanalanalanalanalanala Ditt."

Mrs. Hensworthy surveyed the various creatures standing in her living room. Lorkin appeared rather like a large caterpillar she had recently rooted out of her garden, with various antennae sprouting from what she presumed to be its head; multiple appendages; and standing on its hind, for lack of a better term, legs. The others were no less exotic. She considered shaking hands, but wasn't sure what each of the creatures considered a hand on their bodies. She decided to wave.

"It's a pleasure to meet you all. Perhaps, before you proceed with your inquiries, I might offer you a spot of tea?"

As Lorkin and the others had no idea what constituted 'tea,' they thought the only polite thing to do was to accept the offer, and evaluate the substance upon its arrival. Mrs. Hensworthy started for the kitchen to put the pot on.

"Oh dear, it appears your rift, if that's what you called it, is rather in my way at the moment. I'll just go around to the kitchen entrance in the hallway, and be back in a moment with tea, and perhaps a few biscuits. If you'll be kind enough to wait just a bit."

Brobding Measelfort assured her of their patience, and she heard Lorkin speaking with Brobding, discussing something that sounded like 'Barnork,' as she disappeared into the adjacent hallway. She then entered the kitchen and put a pot of water on the stove.

As she was waiting for the water to boil, she happened to turn to the doorway through the bookcase that accessed the living room from the kitchen side. She had a clear view of the beings in her living room, as well as the furnishings, and the fireplace burning evenly in its locale on the far wall.

"How very odd! It's as if there's nothing out of the ordinary from this side. It appears that I can just walk right back into the living room! Perhaps I'll inquire of that nice Mr. Measelfort first, to make sure I don't disturb their rift or whatever it is they're so concerned about. Oh, Mr. Measelfort!"

Brobding heard Mrs. Hensworthy calling from the kitchen. The sound appeared to emanate from behind the rift. "How may I help, Mrs. Hensworthy?"

"I was just wondering, dear, if I should disturb any of your nice things if I were to walk through the bookcase and back into the living room. The way appears to be clear from here, and it's a shorter journey, what with the tray of tea and delectables in hand."

Brobding looked somewhat disturbed. "I wouldn't recommend it, Mrs. Hensworthy. While the dimensions are well separated from your perspective, and you therefore can't perceive the intact portion of the transdimensional tube, the outer portion of the rift itself presents as a two dimensional disturbance in your 3-space, and I shouldn't want you to trip on the edge as you make your way past it."

"Understood, dear," although complete clarity on the subject rather eluded her. "I'll come around then."

She returned to the living room with a tray containing a tea service, and various biscuits and cakes.

Her guests watched as she indulged, and followed suit accordingly. Beelox was the first to react.

"What an interesting substance! Rather acidic, I should say; I'm detecting chlorogenic, gallic and phenolic compounds! And you say you ingest this regularly? What a curiosity! And a pleasant flavor!" The others nodded in agreement, except for Nalanalanalanalanala-nala Ditt, whose system did not react particularly well to acidic compounds. She turned an interesting hue of purple, and rather unceremoniously expunged the tea she had ingested back into the cup. "I do apologize, Mrs. Hensworthy; I don't do well with acids."

"I understand, dear; I have the same problem with spicy foods!" She laughed. The others interpreted this correctly as a reflection of some form of joviality, and responded accordingly with various forms of vibration and movement.

Just as they began to explore the biscuits Mrs. Hensworthy had provided, Gwendolyn returned through the front door, with a constable in tow. As Gwendolyn stood there, her mouth once more agape, the constable seemed rather taken aback by what he observed. His mouth opened and closed several times, rather like a fish when removed from the water, before he once again gathered his wits about him.

"What... I.... Ah..... Right! What's all this, then! Mrs. Hensworthy, you should have reported this immediately to the local constabulary! I say, dear oh dear oh dear, I'm sure my chief will have something to say about this! What are all these, all these..... exactly what is transpiring here then, madam!"

Mrs. Hensworthy turned calmly to the gentleman. "Constable Tweedley, you are, as always, a walking cliché; do pull yourself together, man! After all, we have guests here from, I should say, some distance away, and we don't want them to think of us as inhospitable! They've simply come to repair a, what was it again, an interdimensional rift, I believe. Now we really should let them go about their work."

Constable Tweedley was a tall fellow, whose constable's hat made him look even taller. He was quite thin, and wore a thin moustache over his lip. As a matter of fact, essentially everything about the man might be characterized as 'thin.'

Constable Tweedley was speechless for another moment as he surveyed the scene. "I..... Why, I must report this at once to my chief!" With that, Tweedley turned to the door and bolted. Gwendolyn ran after him, yelling something about protecting her aunt from the dastardly aliens. Brobding couldn't help but overhear her comment, and once again tried to offer the benefit of the doubt to these unusual creatures, taking the insult in stride. But it was certainly becoming more of a challenge.

# 8

Some time later, the Earth had rotated nominally on its axis, and advanced nominally in its orbit. The sun appeared to be in a nominally different position relative to the horizon. And Mrs. Hensworthy had removed the tea things.

Lorkin Lort and his associates were proceeding to examine the rift in an animated fashion, chattering away excitedly. Meanwhile, Brobding Measelfort was methodically preparing a carefully-blended quantity of transdimensional concrete, in order to repair the rift as soon as Lorkin and his team were finished with their evaluation. Mrs. Hensworthy was enjoying another cup of tea in front of the fire, and watching with interest the various activities in her living room.

The front door opened once again; Gwendolyn had returned with reinforcements. Not only had she continued to involve poor Constable

Tweedley, but now his superior, Chief Constable Broadkirk, made an appearance.

Chief Constable Broadkirk was a rather short and portly fellow, perhaps in his early fifties in Earth years. Surprisingly, the same hat that made Constable Tweedley look taller somehow made Chief Constable Broadkirk look, well, broader. It was clear from his physique that the Chief Constable spent rather too much time in the Chief Constable's chair at the station house, and not nearly enough time perambulating about the village. He could be overheard berating Constable Tweedley as they made their way through the door, to the effect of, "You better not be wasting my time again, Tweedley. You know, I have better things to do than chase down Mrs. Hensworthy's wild imaginings. I hope she isn't accusing the neighborhood cat of stealing the laundry off her line again. She really needs to…." His voice trailed off as he entered the living room and observed the collection of beings working away therein. He stood near the hallway entrance to the room, temporarily speechless. His eyes seemed rather wider than usual.

Mrs. Hensworthy observed him entering the room. "Ah, Chief Constable Broadkirk, won't you join me for a cup of tea? Allow me to introduce my guests. Although I'd suggest allowing them to offer you one of these little widgets for your nose first; it makes conversation with them ever so much more interesting."

The Chief Constable recovered his ability to speak shortly thereafter. "For my nose?! For my NOSE?! Mrs. Hensworthy, what in the name of Hades is transpiring here! You appear to have a variety of enormous insects in your living room! I don't know if I should be contacting the military, or an exterminator!"

These comments were getting to be a bit much, even for Brobding Measelfort, who was the most congenial fellow in the room. He just couldn't help himself; he had to comment.

"Mrs. Hensworthy, I presume this is a fellow member of your species. As it doesn't currently have a GadgiYack in place, would you be kind enough to let it know that I shall patch the interdimensional rift as soon as Professor Lort and his colleagues have completed their studies, and we shall therefore be leaving your dimension in short order. We certainly shouldn't wish to impose upon your hospitality."

Mrs. Hensworthy offered a smile. "Please, Mr. Measelfort, it's no imposition at all, I can assure you! I rather welcome the refreshing company of you and your associates!" She then turned to Chief Constable Broadkirk.

"Chief Constable, that will be quite enough, thank you very much! You've insulted my guests, and I shant have it, I tell you! If you'd care to be civil, I shall allow you to remain; otherwise, please return to your other duties; I don't particularly care for your tone."

Chief Constable Broadkirk's rather round face began to resemble the tomatoes in Mrs. Hensworthy's garden, turning various shades of red as he absorbed the woman's comments. When he was once again more or less in control of his emotions, and his cheeks had resumed a relatively normal tonal shade, he replied through gritted teeth, "Mrs. Hensworthy, I shall be returning forthwith with a heavily armed contingent from the local military reserve, in order to scour these creatures from our midst! Until then, I should take care, madam, as their dinner hour may be approaching, and they may decide to make you their main course! Come along, Tweedley!" With that, the Chief Constable made for the door, wearing a notable scowl, with Constable Tweedley following closely behind him like a well-trained canine.

Gwendolyn stood there watching the proceedings, and was unable to comprehend how her aunt was so calm in the midst of what Gwendolyn perceived to be an alien invasion.

"Aunt Eleanora, what exactly is happening here?! I really don't understand how it is you're taking this all in stride. I mean, really, Auntie! There are giant bugs in your living room, for goodness sakes!" Needless to say, we've paraphrased dear Gwendolyn's comments, so as not to offend our more sensitive readers. Brobding did his best to ignore yet another insulting barb thrown in his direction.

Mrs. Hensworthy calmly sipped her tea as she listened to Gwendolyn's rant. "Gwendolyn, dear, do sit down; there's something I suppose I should tell you, so you stop all this nonsense about 'aliens.'"

Gwendolyn sat down on the sofa, glancing occasionally at the various creatures working behind her, in case one of them decided to once again attempt to incorrectly install a GadgiYack in the wrong orifice. Mrs. Hensworthy continued.

"As you know, dear, your Uncle Malthorp departed some time ago for points unknown. There's something of interest that you never knew about Uncle Malthorp. You see, about 25 years ago, I heard rather an odd sound emanating from my back garden, and discovered a very strange little vessel parked in the vicinity of the garden shed. In turns out that Uncle Malthorp had strayed through another one of these interdimensional rifts or some such with his flying doodad, and landed in my garden in order to consult a map, or chart, or however these flying sort refer to their local tourist guidebook."

"You see, Uncle Malthorp was from a planet quite some distance from here, and quite possibly in another dimensional space; oh, he tried to explain it to me several times, but it was all very much beyond me. He was an unusual fellow; I believe he used the term "shape shifter," or something of that ilk. He was more or less a gelatinous blob when he first emerged from his vessel, and I must say, my first reaction to an alien was similar to your own! But, he was holding some gadget that allowed us to speak with each other, and after a bit of conversation and a nice cup of tea, I found him to be most agreeable company."

"After perusing my library, Malthorp reformulated himself into something closer to human form, and I offered him a pair of my garden slacks and a fairly androgynous blouse to wear. He really looked quite human after that, and we had a lovely time together."

"As he couldn't quite manage to find that rift again, and slip back into his own universe, or whatever space he came from, I offered to accommodate him. One thing led to another, and we had a lovely 20 years together. Of course, for Malthorp, that was just the blink of an eye; apparently his species lives for hundreds and hundreds of our years."

"He slipped off about five years ago, mumbling something about having to molt; I'm afraid I don't know where he is at the moment, poor dear. I suppose he'll find his way back after he's molted, or whatever it is he needs to do."

"So perhaps now you understand why I don't find these visitors particularly disturbing. Is there anything you would like to ask me, dear?"

Gwendolyn sat with her mouth agape, unsure as to how she should react to this news. "Auntie! You lived with an alien for 20 years?! Weren't you worried that he might, I don't know, do as the Chief Constable mentioned, and enjoy you for dinner one night?!"

Mrs. Hensworthy smiled and enjoyed another sip of her tea. "Oh, Gwendolyn dear, do grow a pair, as they say, and enjoy a little adventure! Malthorp was completely harmless, as are these lovely beings keeping us company at the moment. Most of these creatures just want to get on with their lives, and have a little joy now and then, just like anyone. And, I should mention quite confidentially," she added as she leaned toward Gwendolyn and spoke in a voice barely more than a whisper, "that the shape shifting ability did offer certain *very* distinct advantages when Malthorp and I enjoyed our weekly romp!" Mrs. Hensworthy smiled rather broadly.

Gwendolyn positively cringed. "Oh, Auntie! Oh, dear! Oh my! I don't want to hear about it!" She covered her ears in anticipation of her aunt further relating such intimate details.

Before Mrs. Hensworthy could finish another sip of tea, Lorkin Lort approached.

"Mrs. Hensworthy, we've completed our evaluation of this rift, and will be departing shortly. We wanted to bid you farewell, and thank you for your understanding and lovely hospitality."

"Not at all, Professor Lort; it was my pleasure to have you in my home. I presume we won't be having any more visitors through my bookcase after you're through?"

Brobding Measelfort spoke up. "There will be no issue there, Mrs. Hensworthy; I'll make certain that the interdimensional rift is properly repaired, and you shouldn't have any further interruptions."

Lorkin and his colleagues waved a collection of appendages as they once again stepped through the rift, and back into the transdimensional transport tube. Brobding Measelfort added some similar departing comments to the ladies as he too made his exit, and began his final repairs to the tube wall.

As Lorkin was thinking to himself that perhaps that report on the indigenous species here was not completely accurate with respect to their rather barbaric nature, the front door opened once more. A very official-looking fellow marched in a very military fashion through the opening, along with far too many additional soldiers, and some rather ominous looking equipment. Considering the crowd, they barely fit in the living room. Chief Constable Broadkirk and Constable Tweedley could be seen through the open doorway, observing the proceedings from some, and I daresay what they considered a safe, distance away.

The official-looking fellow looked nervously about the room. He saw Mrs. Hensworthy and her niece sitting before the fire, and caught sight of Brobding Measelfort as he worked methodically to complete his repairs. The official-looking fellow began to speak in an official-sounding fashion.

"Madam, I am Sergeant Major DeLade Greene of the North Yorkshire Regiment, at your service. I have been informed by the local constabulary of an apparent alien infestation in your living room, and I see that the information was in fact correct! You should have informed us immediately, madam! Immediately, I say!" He looked rather sternly at Mrs. Hensworthy, who continued to enjoy her tea.

Without waiting for her response, he turned to his squad. "Right lads. Corporal Smithers, bring forth the RPG; that's a good lad. We'll have this issue resolved for you in a moment's time, madam, a moment's time, I say. Right then, target at 2 o'clock, fire when ready!"

Brobding Measelfort was paying no attention to the activities in the living room. He carefully applied the last of the transdimensional concrete to the rift, and of a sudden, it was as if the rift had never existed. The passage to Mrs. Hensworthy's kitchen was fully restored, with no evidence of any dimensional disturbance whatsoever. The dimensions were once again separate and distinct.

Of course, Sergeant Major Greene failed to notice this, and perhaps did not care to notice this, as he gave the order to fire. Before Mrs. Hensworthy could utter a single word, a projectile was launched through her bookcase, and proceeded to utterly demolish the far wall of her kitchen, obliterating several of her favorite potted plants in the process.

# 9

As Lorkin Lort and his associates made their way back to The Center for Education in the Galactic Sciences on Lechien 7, to prepare their report on the interdimensional rift, Brobding Measelfort slowly and carefully completed his repair. Because the rift was now completely sealed, and he was no longer exposed to Barnork 3's 3-space, he was completely unaware of Sergeant Major Greene's rather over-the-top reaction to his presence.

Brobding made a note of the location; he had a feeling that he might like to return to Mrs. Hensworthy's living room at some future date. She was a very hospitable host, and Brobding found that odd acidic substance *tea* quite enjoyable. As he was an expert on transdimensional tube breaches, Brobding thought to himself, he would have no trouble opening and closing the occasional interdimensional doorway for a visit.

A thought suddenly occurred to him. "Oh, goodness, I forgot to retrieve the GadgiYack from Mrs. Hensworthy! Well, now I *will* need to visit again soon!" The various technicians of the MITE Corporation had been told not to introduce new technologies to species that were not yet at an advanced level of technological prowess, and, with respect to technology, the humans clearly were some distance behind the proverbial times. For the moment, he proceeded with his work. When he was finished, the casual passerby couldn't even tell there had been a breach in that section of the tube.

Lorkin and his cohort completed their evaluation, and he connected once more with Porlot Wheezleween for a closing discussion on the matter. Her Primary Brain Section was all ears, so to speak.

"We were extraordinarily fortunate that this rift occurred in a location that offered compatible atmosphere as well as matter volume. Otherwise, we might have had a serious decompression in the tube. What might have been even worse, and I hesitate to even ponder it, would have been a substantial interdimensional transfer of matter, with possible extraordinary consequences for nearby planetary systems, given the gravitational imbalances that might have been introduced." Just describing such a scenario caused Lorkin to shudder.

Porlot was just glad to get some resolution around the whole affair. "I appreciate your feedback, Lorkin. We still have a few small breaches to clean up, but, barring any further accidents, I think we've seen the last of these unplanned rifts."

"We've been in discussion with representatives of the Planetarial Movement. As it so happens, the Planetarial's complaints weren't entirely unfounded. Many of the competing products that motivated their isolationist perspective, as well as their rather militant behaviors, were being subsidized by the governments on the companies' home planets. In exchange for the Planetarial's moratorium on this breach business, we've agreed to convene a system-wide interplanetary roundtable to negotiate the systematic removal of government subsidies over a relatively short time frame, thus leveling the planetary playing field for foot fungus powder, among many other products. I'm sure the companies that had wrangled those subsidies out of their representatives won't be particularly happy, but with various elections coming up across the network, it will give the incumbents some worthwhile reductions in government expenditure to brag about with their populations. So, good show all around."

# 10

Sergeant Major DeLade Greene surveyed the destruction he had just brought about. "Oh, I say, I say, well done, Smithers! Good show all around!"

To understate it rather dramatically, Mrs. Hensworthy wore a look of horror as she stared in the direction of what was formerly her kitchen.

"Sergeant Major, what do you have to say for yourself?!" Mrs. Hensworthy had noticeably lost her cordial tone. "You utterly laid waste to Maurice, my favorite philodendron plant, to say nothing of the disaster you've created in what was once my kitchen!"

The Sergeant Major continued to survey the scene with a look of what can only be described as pride. "Now, now, madam, cost of war and all that sort. You must agree, we've cleared up that alien infestation rather nicely! No sign of them whatsoever! I think we can safely say they won't be bothering you any further, no they shall not!  Not after they've had a taste of Sergeant Major Greene and his top notch regiment.  All right, lads, back to base!"  With that, the Sergeant Major turned to go, preceded by the many soldiers who had simply stood around earlier to watch the activities unfold.

Mrs. Hensworthy was far from satisfied.  She called after him as he departed, "You haven't heard the last of this!  Colonel Messington is a close acquaintance, and we shall be having words!!"  But the words dissipated in the evening air; the Sergeant Major was already in what appeared to be a small armored vehicle, and on his way out of the village.

Some months later, after considerable traffic on the proverbial line among Mrs. Hensworthy, Colonel Messington, and The Right Honourable Fern Horseley, MP for Harrogate, Hampsthwaite and the adjacent villages that dotted the Yorkshire countryside, Sergeant Major Greene had been reassigned, through a little known exchange program, to a governmental liaison office in Escasoni, Nova Scotia, Canada; he was last seen shopping for fleece-lined parkas at one of the local shoppes.  Meanwhile, Mrs. Hensworthy was enjoying a new kitchen, a new conservatory off the back of the cottage, and a new philodendron that she named Penelope, because it reminded her of a Penelope with whom she'd attended school some time ago.

For Mrs. Hensworthy, all that nonsense with Sergeant Major DeLade Greene was but a distant memory, and she had returned to enjoying her afternoon tea, with a pleasant afternoon fire burning in the fireplace.

Some short time hence, she was ensconced in just such a scenario when, of a sudden, her front door opened once more, and, after missing for over five years, her dearly departed husband Malthorp appeared in the living room...

<<<<>>>>

*Stay tuned for the next exciting chapter...*

B

www.ingramcontent.com/pod-product-compliance
Lightning Source LLC
Chambersburg PA
CBHW071342130626
46556CB00005B/1991